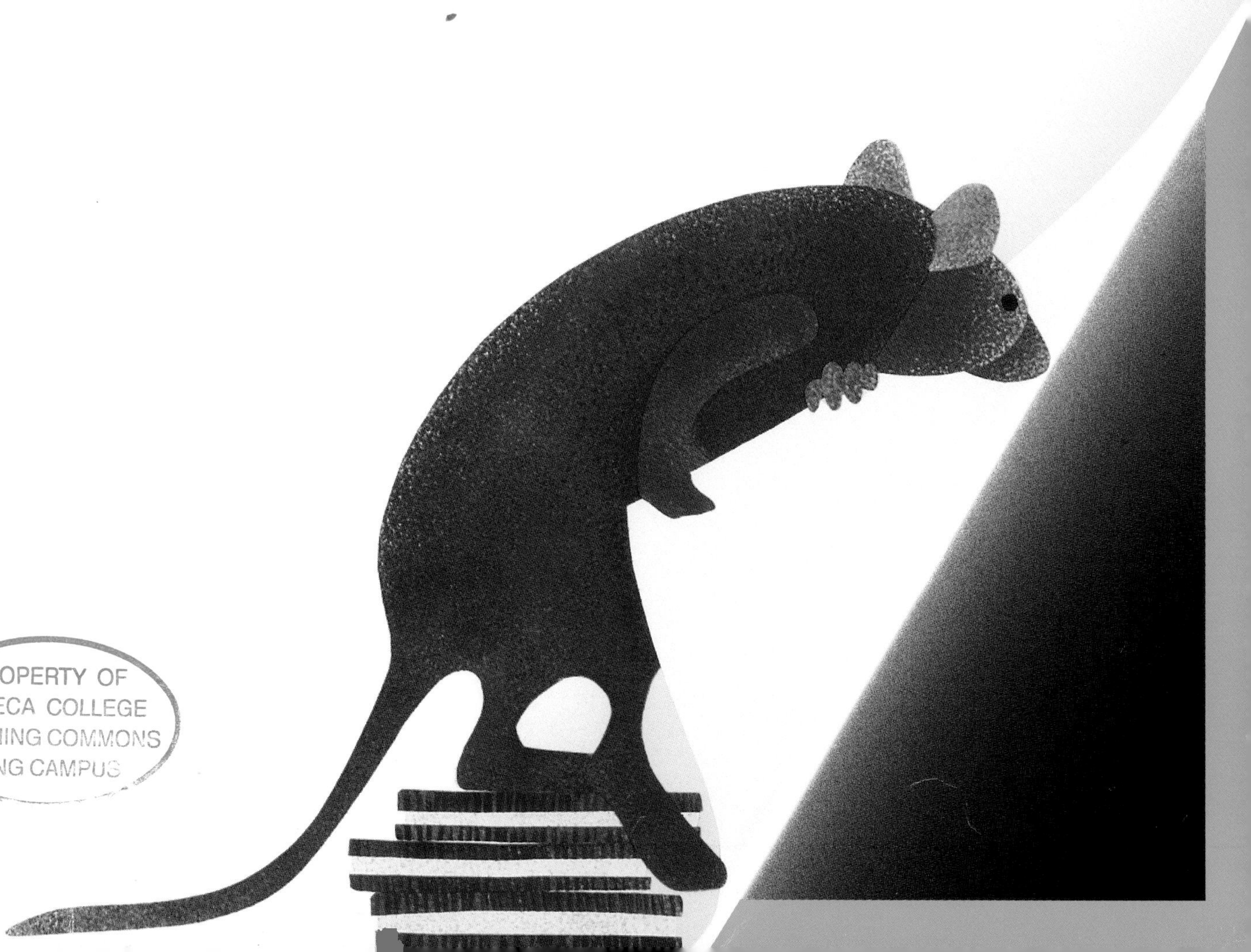

MOUSE

LINNEA RILEY

MESS

THE BLUE SKY PRESS

An Imprint of Scholastic Inc. · New York

THE BLUE SKY PRESS

Permissions Department,

The Blue Sky Press, an imprint of Scholastic Inc.,

557 Broadway, New York, New York 10012.

The Blue Sky Press is a registered trademark of Scholastic Inc.

Library of Congress Cataloging-in-Publication Data

Riley, Linnea Asplind.

Mouse mess / Linnea Asplind Riley.   p.   cm.

Summary: A hungry mouse leaves a huge mess
when it goes in search of a snack.

ISBN 0-590-10048-3

[1. Mice—Fiction.   2. Food—Fiction.]   I. Title.

PZ7.R4555Mo   1997   [E]—dc21   96-49499   CIP   AC

20 19 18 17 16 15 14

Printed in Mexico   49

First printing, October 1997

Production supervision by Angela Biola

Designed by Linnea Riley and Kathleen Westray

For my dad who loves…

Hush, hush, a little mouse

is sound asleep inside his house.

On the stairs, the sound of feet!

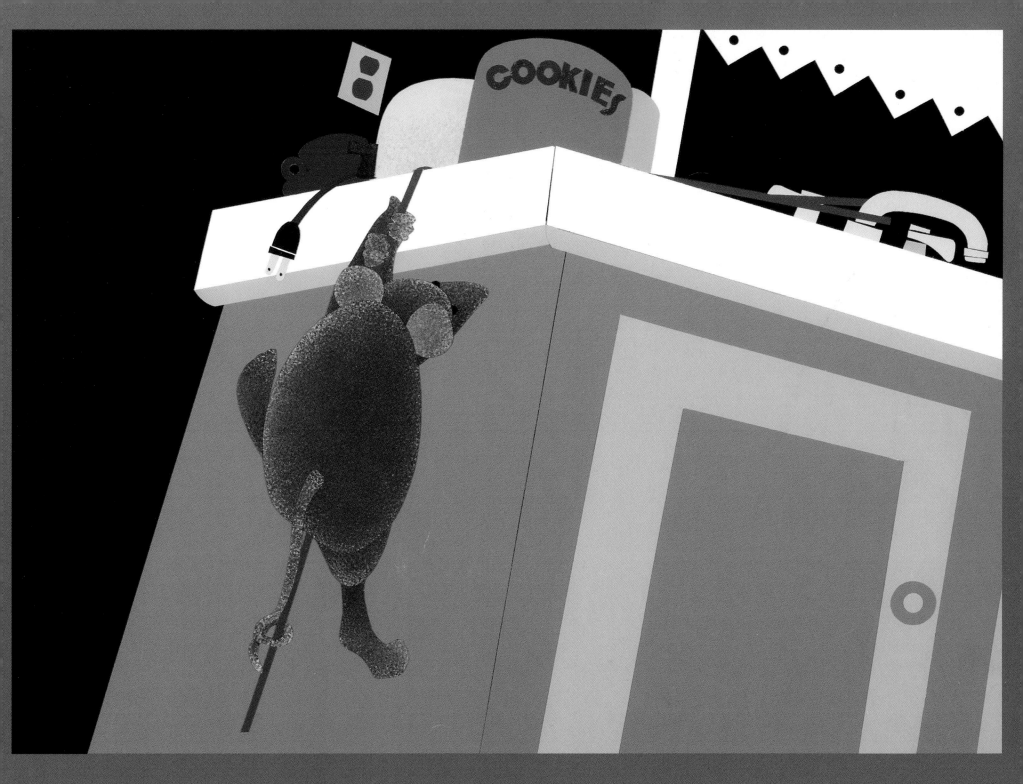

Mouse is up. It's time to eat!

Crunch-crunch, he wants a cracker.

Munch-munch, a cookie snacker.

Crackle-sweep, he rakes corn flakes

and jumps into the pile he makes.

Sniff-sniff, milk and cheese.

Mouse would like a taste of these.

Splish-splash, the milk spills out.

Food is scattered all about.

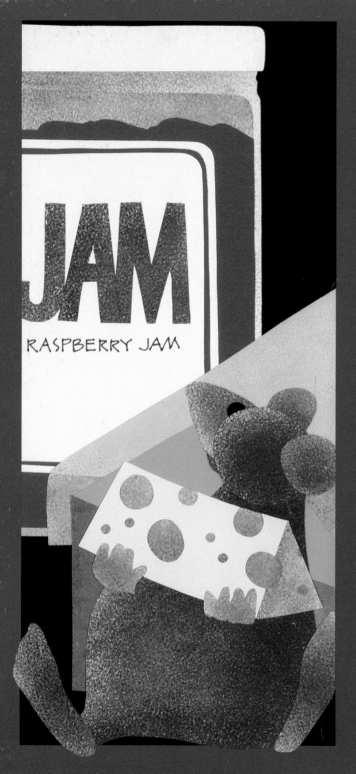

Sticky-gooey, jam to spread

with peanut butter smeared on bread.

Tipping, slipping, sugar falls.

Pour and pat, make castle walls.

Olives, pickles, catsup—fun!

Pop the tops off, one by one!

Mouse steps back. He looks around.

He can't believe the mess he's found.

"Who made   this awful mess?" asks Mouse.

"These   people need to clean their house!"

Gurgle, bubble, water flows,

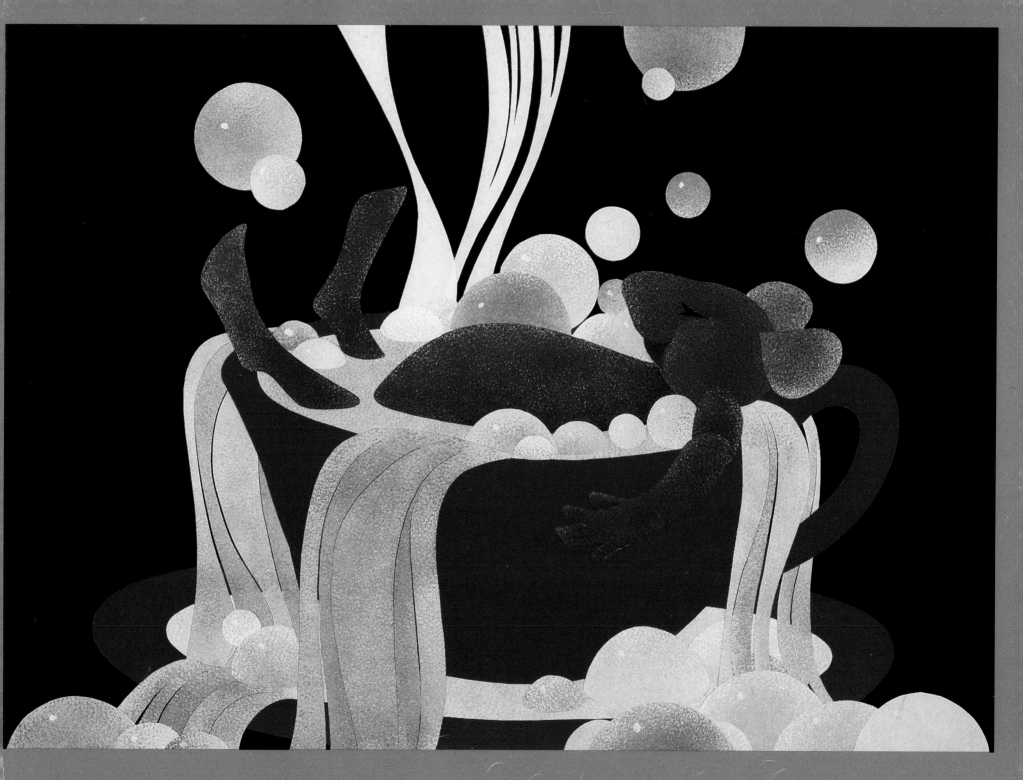

soaks the jam between his toes.

Now that Mouse is clean and fed,

he leaves the mess and goes...

to bed!